THE DREAM
THIEF

T. R. ROSS

Winter Wolf
PUBLICATIONS
TRIMOON
ECLIPSE
/ Cincinnati, OH

Copyright © 2021, Tracy Renée Ross
Cover art and design © 2021, by Miriam Chowdhury
Interior art © 2021, by Miriam Chowdhury
Edited by James Daniel Ross
Interior Design by Tracy Renée Ross

Published by TriMoon Eclipse,
An imprint of Winter Wolf Publications, LLC

ISBN: 978-1-945039-21-8 (paperback)

Forward

For many years now I have wanted to write a book for my younger readers. I can't tell you how many parents and teachers have approached me, all asking about my books and if I have any that are suited for children. It was always with sadness in my heart that I had to tell them 'no'. It took me a long time to find a reason to write for children, more than just adults telling me they want me to. I needed to find that take-away, that message in a bottle, that significance a child could derive from a really good book. And then, one day, it was like magic. It was right there in my head, ready to be tapped, eager to be put into words. I wanted it to be unique without being too unusual, believable with an element of the fantastical, understandable, thought-provoking, and above all else, entertaining.

Growing up, I was enamored with felines, both big and small. Any book I could get my hands on that was about cats, I would read it. Any movies, and I would watch them. In almost every one, cats were portrayed as a bit peculiar, often mysterious, and sometimes downright odd. But one of the things that really caught my attention was the way ancient Egyptians believed cats were magical creatures capable of bringing good luck to the people who housed them. And as it turned out, other cultures around the world also view cats in a favorable light, even going so far as to say they are protectors against evil spirits. That idea is played out in many movies and books, shown by the way that cats will often stare as if they are intently watching something, something that is not visible to anyone else.

As a young girl, things were difficult for me. My father worked for a company that required him to move around a lot, so in elementary school, I was always the new kid in class. I was a daydreamer, and shy. I was never one to conform, so I didn't really fit in. My teachers were constantly reminding me to get my head out of the clouds, and the other kids were taunting me about how weird I was. As the years progressed, it was increasingly difficult to make friends. I had a vivid imagination, so nightmares were part of my nightly dreamscape.

The Dream Thief

This was all on top of the myriad of issues that any child goes through as they proceed through life.

So, it was with these ideas in mind that I developed the basis for The Dream Thief. This book will be the launching pad upon which I will write all of my future books in the Cat Tales series. All will feature feline friends that walk through life with the children they love, children that are experiencing all of the tough things life has to throw at them on any given day. They will also feature bravery, determination, faithfulness, friendship, and above all, love.

It is my sincerest desire that you enjoy this book. Thank you for your time and support, and happy reading!

Tracy

Chapter 1

I sat, huddled, in the back corner of the barred space I'd called home since I arrived at his place. The floor and walls were cold and hard, unforgiving. Scents <u>assailed</u> my nostrils, mostly those of the other cats that were there in the room with me, and underlying all of those, a chemical smell that made me sneeze. In the distance I could hear the sound of dogs barking. The sound never <u>ceased</u> until the night came and the lights went out, plunging me into darkness. It was a terrifying place, and I dreamed of the day I could be free of it.

The door of the room opened and the sound of the barking grew louder for a moment before it closed again. It was replaced by the sound of human voices. "All of the cats have had their <u>vaccinations</u>, and have passed their wellness exams," said a familiar voice. It was the woman who came to feed me at the beginning and end of every day, the same one who cleaned my litter pan and petted my fur.

"Do you have any females?" asked another voice, one I'd never heard before. By the sound, I could tell it was another woman.

"Yes, they are all over here," said the familiar voice.

The two women came close to the bars of my space, accompanied by a big man with hair on his face. They took some time to look through all of the other spaces before they came to mine.

"Ahhh! A tiger-striped calico! She's beautiful!" said the unfamiliar woman.

The latch to my space clicked open and the bars swung away. A familiar hand presented itself to me, and I purred despite my nervousness. The familiar woman picked me up and brought me out, placing me into a stranger's arms. A mildly floral scent made my whispers twitch as the new woman brought me face to face with her. Hazel eyes sparkled warmly as she gazed into mine. Her face was round, framed by shoulder-length light brown hair, and her lips pulled into a delighted grin.

The Dream Thief

"And her eyes are such a vivid green and blue!" she said.

A feeling of vulnerability swept over me and my tail curled instinctively between my hind legs. The ordeal of the past few days flooded my mind and I trembled in her grasp, uncertainty settling into my bones. But the woman brought me close to her chest, curved her arms around me in a protective embrace. The floral scent was stronger here, and it enveloped me.

"What should we name her?" she looked up at the man with the hairy face.

The man chuckled, a deep soothing sound. "I think Freya would suit her."

The woman's arms tightened briefly. "Oh, yes! I love it!"

T.R. ROSS

Chapter 2

Surrounded by a gentle <u>drone,</u> I huddled within the dark enclosed space. The floor was plush, the sides soft and giving. It reminded me of other such enclosures I'd experienced before, but without the hardness all around. This space felt nice, and my elbows and knees sank into the cushion beneath. I could pick up the scent of another cat that had once been sheltered there. It was a male. Unease made my guts churn. Male cats often meant trouble, and I'd already had enough of that.

Suddenly there was a bump, swiftly followed by another. The hum I'd been enjoying <u>abruptly</u> stopped. There was a click and a rush of cool air swept into my space through the small holes on the top and sides. There was the sound of a door closing, the disorienting sensation of being moved, the crunch of footsteps in the leaves.

Another click and I was once more in a warm place. New, exciting smells overwhelmed my nose, and when I was set down, I crept towards the front of my small space. I looked out of the bars to see a big room that had a fireplace with happy flames dancing within. There were big brown sofas, a throw rug on the polished wood floor, and...

...and a strange cat coming straight towards me.

He was huge, easily twice my size, and his fur was a glossy silver gray. But above all, his most distinguishable characteristic was the one golden eye he had fixed on me as he moved closer and closer. The other eye was simply not there, the socket puckered up and closed shut. My <u>hackles</u> began to rise and I felt it before I heard it, the growl that rumbled deep within my chest before making it to my throat.

"Raawwwr!"

The one-eyed cat <u>ambled</u> to a stop and sat back on his <u>haunches</u>, the tip of his tail twitching at his side. The woman's singsong voice penetrated my haze of fear, "Now Odin, be extra gentle with this one. You might need all your charm with her!" A hand stroked the top of his head before disappearing again, followed by receding footsteps.

The Dream Thief

I stared at him, daring him to come nearer, my most threatening hiss ready to <u>intimidate</u> him into keeping his distance. But instead, Odin settled down onto his belly and sprawled out on the floor. I cocked my head to the side, wondering. *What's he sitting there for?*

Thump, thump, thump. A <u>cacophony</u> of sound struck my ears and I jerked. Heart racing in my chest, I shrank to the back of my space, crouching low. Laughter filled the living room, followed by streaks of color outside. "Get back here, Todd! Those are MY ear buds!"

"Nuh-uh! They're mine, Ben. Dad said so!"

"C'mon guys, cut it out. I wanna finish our game," said a third boy's voice.

This home belonged to these boys, and several other people. I could smell their scents everywhere. The boys started to argue in <u>earnest</u> as I sat there and listened. Odin was gone, having wisely <u>vacated</u> the area just as the boys burst in.

A shadow hovered over my space for a moment before a fourth boy sat down beside me. I trembled as he unzipped the top of my space, the flap pulling back to reveal a boy younger than the others. His skin was bronzed gold and his hair so dark it looked black. Brown eyes filled with joy as he took me in, his finely sculpted lips curving into a wide smile. He slowly reached in a hand, fingers stretching until they touched the top of my head.

He gave a soft gasp and whispered, "You must be Freya. You're such a pretty girl!"

I perked up at the sound of his voice. Right away I could tell this boy was different from the others. Maybe it was the way he smelled, or maybe it was the gentleness of his touch. Maybe it was the way he looked at me, his smile reaching his eyes to make them twinkle. Maybe it was all three.

The boy reached in further, his hands grasping around me. And just as effortlessly as the woman had earlier that day, he plucked me out of the space. He immediately placed me close to his chest, flipped me over onto my back, and cradled me in his arms.

The Dream Thief

Images swept through my mind: another place, another boy. *He held me tightly in his arms, his soft kisses raining down onto my head, face, and paws. His giggles filled my ears, sweet sounds that I wanted to hear forever. His blue eyes shimmered with such happiness it filled my soul and made it soar.*

I blinked. The images faded away and I was looking at brown eyes instead of blue, black hair instead of blond. That other boy was gone, long gone. Sadness welled within me until the new boy leaned down, his lips brushing against my nose. "I've only just met you, but I love you already," he whispered.

T.R. ROSS

Chapter 3

I sat atop the navy blue comforter, watching as the new boy prepared for rest. He dressed quickly, then sat beside me on the bed, petting me over my head and back. I purred in contentment, <u>luxuriating</u> in the attention, then lay down. He took the cue and slid beneath the covers, pulling them up to his chin. A floral scent <u>wafted</u> through the air as the woman came into the room, and he gave her a wide smile. "Freya wants to sleep with me tonight, Ma!"

She sat on the edge of the bed. "She does?"

The boy nodded enthusiastically. "Maybe she will keep the Boogeyman out of my room!"

Ma gave him a sidelong look. "Oh Sam! You know there's no such thing!"

"But Ma, I TOLD you-"

"I'll have to put a litter box in here for her then, just in case. It's a new house and she won't know where to go," she interrupted.

Sam gave a little squeal of delight. "Ok!"

I looked around as the two continued to talk, my gaze drawn to the open doorway. Odin sat there, his tail wrapped around his feet, staring at me out of his one golden eye. I narrowed my gaze as he <u>sauntered</u> into the room, rubbing against Ma's leg as she left.

"Odin, come here boy! Let me show you to Freya." Sam leaned down and patted the covers hanging along the side of the bed. "Come on, boy!"

Odin approached the bed and <u>vaulted</u> atop it, rubbing his head along Sam's hand and arm as the boy petted him. Sam then scooped the large <u>tom</u> into his arms and scooted towards me. I rose from my place, hackles rising, my eyes widening with alarm just as Ma suddenly called from downstairs. "Sam, come down for a moment! You forgot to put your dinner plate in the sink!"

Sam rolled his eyes as he released Odin, scrambling out of the bed and rushing out of the room to do Ma's bidding. Meanwhile, the other cat looked at me, his whiskers twitching with amusement. I gave him a <u>disdainful</u> glare, followed by a hiss. His whiskers twitched again. "So you are

The Dream Thief

THE Freya the humans keep talking about. Heh, you don't LOOK very troublesome."

I intensified my glare, wondering what they had possibly been saying about me. *Trouble?*

Odin stepped closer, his long tail swaying sinuously behind him. "You look more like a scaredy cat."

I growled deep in my throat, warning him to keep his distance, not bothering to issue a response, my back rising defensively.

"Calm down, darling. I'm not here to fight with you." He preened for a moment. "Though if we did fight, I'd win."

I hissed again at his choice of words. "Then why ARE you here?"

He cocked his head. "As I recall, you are in my territory."

I blinked, recognizing his words as truth, and forced myself to back down despite my instincts screaming at me to remain in the offensive. I was in a strange house, with stranger inhabitants. I didn't see how this could possibly go well.

Odin kept his eye on me, his tail flicking in acknowledgement of my <u>concession</u>. "I noticed you have chosen Sam to be your boy."

I raised my chin, defying him to tell me I couldn't.

"Likewise, he has chosen you to be his cat." Odin's tone shifted, became almost pleading. "Don't let him down."

I blinked, not expecting his heartfelt statement. For a moment all I could do was stand there before giving a flick of my tail. "I won't."

Odin finally took his eye off me and sat back on his haunches. "Good, now that's established, time to fill you in."

I continued to stand there, almost defiant. "Fill me in on what?"

"There's something <u>amiss</u> in this house. The only human who can sense it is Sam."

The Dream Thief

Chapter 4

I slunk silently in the deep shadows cast by the moonlight streaming in through the window, my eyes scanning the dark room. Sam slept peacefully, his chest rising and falling with his breaths, one hand clutched around the stuffed toy Ma had given him from the small pile neatly organized in the far corner. Near the bed was a nightstand with a lamp, and beyond that, a large desk topped with shelves filled with those small rectangular things that humans liked to stare at for extended periods of time. Alongside it was a table, and atop that was a big glass box. I leapt up beside it, placing my forepaws on the side and looking in. I crinkled my nose at the strangeness of the smell, but stayed to watch as the shell situated in the center of the box grew a head that extended up to stare at me through small black eyes.

I leapt back down to the floor again, prowling about beneath the bed and into the cavernous closet. I found a nice perch within and sat there for several moments, just taking in what lay beyond. My gaze continued to be drawn to the desk on the opposite wall, the one with the tall shelves. I looked up, the height of them making my skin tense with anticipation.

I wanted to climb it.

I trotted over and leapt onto the desk, taking one shelf at a time, careful not to knock anything over, until I reached the very top. And there I teetered for a breath, gaining my footing before turning to look down. This time, when I sat there and looked around, I was satisfied.

I continued my <u>nocturnal</u> prowl, sneezing on the dust motes I stirred with my passing. My whiskers twitched as I once more smelled something unfamiliar. I looked down at the strange creature in the glass box. No, it was different than that, a <u>caustic</u> one that made my <u>olfactory</u> sense recoil. I followed the scent where it led up the wall towards the ceiling, standing on my hind legs to follow where the trail led.

And then it simply disappeared.

I regarded the wall <u>quizzically</u>. There was nothing out of the ordinary about it. It was just a

The Dream Thief

simple wall, painted blue, that met an off-white ceiling that went nowhere.

Not long after, I curled up on Sam's bed near his feet. I watched the boy as he slept. His face was flawless in the pale moonlight, all lines smoothed away by the <u>ethereal</u> glow.

"His sleep is troubled.   The humans call it 'nightmares'."

Odin's words came to my mind as my eyelids drooped.   As of yet, I'd seen no indication of anything being wrong with the boy. He slept the sleep of an angel...

I awoke to the sound of whimpering. My half-open, wandering eyes took in the room, exactly as I'd left it, and then the boy, who moved in his sleep.

Sam whimpered again, his brow beaded with sweat. My whiskers quivered and I sniffed the air. A thick cloud of fear hung there. *Is he dreaming? Is it the nightmare that Odin spoke about?* My senses sprang to wakefulness and it was then I smelled something more– the strange scent from earlier in the evening near the ceiling. I rose from my spot and <u>honed</u> in on it. Sam began to move more, his legs thrashing beneath the covers. The hairs along my back and tail rose, and my claws extended. I stared into the darkness beside Sam's head, noticing something moving there. I stared harder and harder.

And then I saw it.

A shadow stood there beside Sam's pillow. Slanted eyes glowed eerily red in the darkness, and it loomed over the boy's face, doing something. Sam's thrashing intensified, and when he opened his mouth to cry out, a soft yellow glow emerged.

Dumbstruck, I stood there for a moment, taking in the scene. The glow streamed forth, sparkling in the wan moonlight. I growled. It came out as a terrible sound, one I'd heard only once before from my mother when she tried to keep me safe. The shadow was suddenly still, staring malevolently at me from ruby eyes.

And then I leapt.

The Dream Thief

Chapter 5

Odin stared at me, his eye unblinking. "You let it get away?"

I sat back on my haunches, <u>affronted</u>. "It was a shadow! Of course, it got away!"

My failure wasn't from lack of trying. I had made quite the <u>ruckus</u>, enough that the whole house heard it and came running. Odin was the first one there, quickly followed by Ma, Dad, and the seven other children.

If Odin could have sighed at me, I believe he would have. "Well, did you see where it went?"

I thought about it, replaying my attack in my mind. I remembered trying to follow the shadow, remembered my eyes going up the tall bookcase towards the ceiling...

Taking in my hesitation, Odin rose from his place. "Come, let's go."

I followed the tom through the big house, over the hardwood floors covered with rugs perfect to lay upon, up the long staircase lined with tall spindles between which a cat could look down and view the goings-on below. The door was left slightly <u>ajar</u>, and we slipped through the small space and entered Sam's room. Odin followed my gaze, trotted over to the desk and leapt atop it the way I had the night before. He then started up the tall bookcase. I watched his lithe silver form, my whiskers twitching with amusement. He was much bigger than I, and I'd barely managed to knock anything over.

But Odin didn't seem to care about that as much as I. Things tumbled off the shelves: misplaced books, picture frames, trophies. They landed on the desk and onto the floor, and I <u>winced</u> when I heard the breaking of glass. Odin was still for a moment, looking towards the doorway and we waited, waited, waited to see if Ma had heard the commotion. When she never came, he continued up to the very top.

Then he looked down, and if cats could smile, I swear he was doing it at that moment.

"Don't tell me you've never been up there before?" I scoffed.

The Dream Thief

He looked <u>abashed</u> and I realized he hadn't. A strange sense of accomplishment came over me. I'd done something in his house during my few hours being there that he'd never done in all the months or years he'd lived there. I vaulted onto the desk and then climbed up to join him. He waved his tail in a gesture of acceptance and contentment, instantly making me relax. We looked down on the room together for a moment. *Maybe we can be friends.* The thought made me feel good.

"So, the shadow went up here. What happened then?" he asked.

"It was dark and hard to see. But it just disappeared."

Odin looked around, putting his nose in the air to sniff. "It smells... strange."

My heart leapt. "Yes! I thought so too."

He followed the smell to the place I did the night before, and with his greater length, his nose just touched the ceiling. He instantly drew back and sneezed. "It smells terrible there."

He was thoughtful for a while before starting back down. I followed, and when we were once more land-bound, I touched him gently with my paw. "So, what now?"

He turned to me, his eye gleaming. "We wait until tonight and capture a shadow."

The Dream Thief

Chapter 6

The boy's fear-filled voice made my heart weep. "Ma, I don't wanna go to bed!"

"Aww, Sam, don't do this to me tonight," Ma replied tiredly, tucking the blankets around him. She glanced around and spied me sitting at the doorway. "And look! Freya is waiting. She wants to sleep with you again." Her voice sounded hopeful and I stood and sauntered into the room.

Sam looked encouraged, and when I leapt up onto the bed, he smiled his beautiful boyish grin that engulfed me in a cocoon of warmth. Ma stroked my fur lovingly for a moment. "You are such a good girl, Freya." She then rose from the bed, stooping to plant a kiss on her son's forehead.

"But what if it comes back tonight?" Sam's whispered voice shook.

Ma put her hand on his face and pitched her voice low. "Remember it's just a dream." She tousled his hair and then turned to leave the room. She paused at the doorway, turned back and gave him a smile. "You are my strong boy, Sammy. I love you." She then turned the light out, closing the door until just a crack remained.

I sat there at Sam's side, my heart struggling through his silent sobs, his hand trembling as he petted me. I loved this boy so much, and I spoke to him a couple times, telling him so. I don't know how much time passed, only that I waited until he finally slipped into slumber, his hand falling to my feet. I licked it, tasting his warm, salty skin, then leapt off the bed. Odin was waiting from me in the depths of the closet where he said he'd be.

Together we <u>nestled</u> there. It was a strange feeling, being so close to another cat. I only <u>vaguely</u> remembered my brothers and sisters, the warmth of them all around me as we curled up next to one another and our mother. I felt a sense of security, my heart beating so close to that of another, and his smell was like none other I'd ever encountered before, rich and <u>robust</u>... wild almost.

We waited, and waited, and waited. The moon rose high in the sky and still we waited. It had been a long day, and the comforting warmth of

The Dream Thief

Odin made me tired. My eyelids drooped, my tail went slack. The darkness pressed all around.

I awoke instantly at the first sound I heard. Odin was alert beside me, his eye trained on the bed. Sam moaned again, a soft sound that told me he was still sleeping. He moved beneath the covers and I tensed, wanting to go to him, tell him it was alright. Odin sensed it and shifted, placing himself in my way. He looked at me, his gaze holding me in place. *Oh yes, I must stay here. I must wait for the shadow to appear,* I thought.

We waited even more. Sam's moaning increased, and his movements. Just when I thought I'd had enough, I saw it. Odin saw it too; I could feel it in the <u>tensing</u> of his muscles where he was pressed against me. The shadow stealthily moved closer, closer, closer, looming higher, higher, higher over my boy, its eyes glowing red in the darkness. Odin silently moved from his place and I followed suit, each of us slowly moving into the places we discussed that afternoon. The pale glow I recalled from the night before started to flow from Sam's open mouth. I <u>hastened</u> my pace, fearful of what that was, what it meant.

Once in place, I looked to where Odin should be, crouched unseen. Then I counted backwards: five, four, three... I saw Odin leap from out of his place. The shadow scurried away, away from Odin and towards the desk. Like they always did during the hunt, my every muscle tightened. TWO... The shadow scaled the shelves, faster than any mouse, vole, or shrew. ONE...

I leapt from my place at the very top, lunging for the shadow. I expected to feel nothing, but to my intense gratification, my open jaws closed down onto a solid form. There was a hideous shriek like nothing I'd ever heard before, nothing of this world. Sharp claws dug into my fur, desperately seeking <u>purchase</u> in the long, thick strands. I could feel it struggling to be free, and I tightened my grip, my teeth sinking deeper into stinking flesh that filled my nostrils and made me want to vomit.

For a moment we grappled there, small hands <u>grasping</u> at my face, seeking to gouge my eyes. It was strong, and I could feel it winning its battle to freedom, pulling itself out of my jaws even as I'd closed them as far as I could. *No, I can't let it get loose! Sam is counting on me!*

And then Odin was there. He grabbed onto the struggling body, his nose touching mine. Another shriek filled the air as he began to pull.

I smiled to myself. I knew this game.

We dug our feet in as best we could on the hard, solid surface of the topmost shelf and played tug o' war with the shadow that wasn't a shadow. We pulled and twisted, Odin's eye gleaming gleefully in the pale moonlight, a low growl rumbling deep in his throat. Finally, there was the tearing of flesh, the popping of bones, and a last gurgling shriek from the thing between us.

And then it was over. We dropped our spoils, and a body lay between us, torn in twain. It was gruesome to behold: sickly, dark green skin, long, pointed ears, a wide mouth filled with tiny razor-sharp teeth, and long arms and legs ending with clawed hands and feet. I rubbed at my face and mouth, the reek of its putrid blood filling my nostrils and resting upon my tongue.

"What is it?" I finally asked.

Odin shook his head. "I don't know, but its dead now."

And just like that, before our very eyes, the thing began to waver and shift. Within moments, laying between us was the mauled remains of a huge, hairy rat.

The lights in the room suddenly clicked on and Ma was there, followed by Dad. "What in the world is going on in here!" she exclaimed.

Sam's excited voice replied. "Ma! You won't believe it! Freya and Odin killed the Boogeyman! It was so cool!"

The Dream Thief

Chapter 7

The family sat around the large dinner table, everyone eating the chicken and rice casserole Ma had made that night for dinner. Odin and I sat in the next room, warming ourselves by the fireplace.

"It was a nasty, fat, rat, okay? There's no such thing as the Boogeyman," said Alex matter-of-factly.

"Yes, there is! I saw it myself!" retorted Sam.

"You were still half asleep," said Todd. "And that rat was a big one. It probably just looked like something else for a few minutes."

Sam frowned. "You weren't there, so you don't know." Sam looked at Ma. "You believe me, don't you?"

There was a pregnant pause before Ma answered. "Well, it's dead and gone now. You can thank the cats for that. I expect it was making lots of noise in the night and that's what you've been hearing. Your sleep should be more restful now."

One of the four girls spoke up, the youngest. "You don't think there are more, do you?" Her eyes were wide with fright.

Ma reached over and patted her shoulder. "Your dad looked all around Sam's room and around the outside of the house. He saw no holes where they could be getting in. So no, I don't believe there are any more, Ranlee."

Odin turned to look at me then, his gaze thoughtful. "I can't believe Dad didn't see it," he said.

"See what?" I asked.

"The hole."

Interest piqued, I sat up. "What hole?"

"The one I saw last night. The shadow rat was making its way there when you caught it."

"Where was it?"

"I'll show you."

We made our way up the stairs and into Sam's room. Once there, Odin looked up at the ceiling

46

near the bookcase. "Up there, the place where we sensed that foul smell," he said.

I narrowed my eyes, looking. "I don't see it."

"I don't either. But it was there last night when the shadow rat was trying to escape us."

"I walked over to the desk, leaped onto the first shelf and began to climb. Once at the top, I caught the faint scent of foulness that got stronger the closer I got to the corner of the wall and the ceiling. I reached as far as I could before settling back down onto my haunches. It was simply too high.

Odin climbed up the bookcase to join me. I moved aside so that he could do the same thing. With his greater length, he was able to touch the corner with his paw. He pulled it back in surprise. "It tingles," he said. He sniffed the paw and made a <u>grimace</u>. "It stinks too."

I also smelled the offending paw and quickly withdrew. "It smells like the shadow rat."

We both looked up at the corner. I imagined a hole there, imagined it opening up...

And that's exactly what happened. Before our eyes, a hole the size of a softball appeared, the edges jagged and undefined, shifting and wavering in the dim lighting of the bedroom.

Odin's eye widened and I imagined my eyes did the same. He crouched low, then sprang upward. His paws caught on the edge of the hole. He hung there for a moment, his back claws scrabbling against the smooth wall for some kind of purchase while he crept forward with the front two. Finally, one back paw reached the mouth of the hole, followed by the other. The hole wavered, stretching to <u>accommodate</u> Odin's body before he disappeared from sight.

"Odin! Odin, are you there?" I called.

His head peeked out of the hole. "I'm here! Come on, it's your turn!"

I crouched low, then thrust myself upward toward the hole. My paws barely touched the edge of the hole before I found myself slipping back down the wall into a heap atop the bookcase, barely keeping myself from falling all the way down to the floor far below.

Odin's tone was encouraging. "Come on, you can do it."

I leaped again, this time with more force. My front paws caught on the edge of the hole and I hung there. I could see inside and it was dark. I could hardly make out the form of Odin. Desperately, I clawed my way forward, my back paws pushing against the wall just like Odin's had.

Then, I felt myself begin to slip.

I dug my claws deeper into the ground and Odin crowded beside me to keep me from slipping more. With a massive heave, I swung my right rear leg up, and it caught the edge. In relief, I scrambled up, felt the cool edges of the hole <u>distort</u> around me as I pulled myself into what appeared to be a long passageway that looked like it stretched into forever.

T.R. Ross

Chapter 8

We didn't walk as long as I'd initially thought we might. The passage slowly spiraled down, down, down, and when we reached the end, we stepped out of the darkness and into a magnificent wood. The trees towered over us in all their majesty, the trunks wider than any I'd ever seen before in all my wanderings before humans took me to live inside of their homes. The leaves were almost as big as me, and colored all the shades of autumn: yellow, orange, red, purple, and everything in between. They formed a thick <u>canopy</u> overhead through which rays of sunlight shone down to touch the ground beneath our feet.

"Where are we?" I asked.

"I don't know, but we aren't home anymore," Odin replied.

"Oh no, you definitely aren't home."

We spun at the unfamiliar singsong voice behind us to find a girl standing there. She looked to be about eleven or twelve years old. Her hair was red, curling past her shoulders down to her slim waist, and her eyes were a <u>vivid</u> shade of blue. She wore a sleeveless light green dress that came to just above her knees. Most enchanting was the pair of semi-transparent wings she had sprouting from her back between her shoulder blades. They glinted in the sunlight as she moved towards us.

"Who are you, and how can you understand what we are saying?" I asked.

She giggled. "Silly kitty, I am Maeve, princess of the fairies, and I can understand all the animals that live here."

"But we don't live here, wherever here is," I said.

Maeve nodded. "I know, but I can understand anyway." She cocked her head. "You are in the Land of the Fairies. Why have you come here?"

"We were following the scent of something that came to our home. It came from here," said Odin.

Maeve nodded. "There are many things from this land that come to your world. They are supposed to keep their presence hidden, and are not allowed to show others the doorways through which they come and go. Most of them are good things."

"Yes, well, this is a bad thing," I said.

"What is it?" asked Maeve.

"We don't know," replied Odin, "but it was giving our boy nightmares and it smelled bad."

Maeve nodded sadly. "Yes, those are goblins. "Unfortunately, they are part of the balance that makes it possible for all of the good things to continue coming through."

"Balance?" I asked.

"Yes, everything must have a balance," replied Maeve. "Otherwise, chaos ensues. It is the same in your world as well, I imagine."

"What was it doing to our boy? It looked terrible," I said.

"It was feeding on his good dreams, leaving behind only the bad. It's why your boy has only the nightmares every night. He has no good dreams to counter them."

"Well, it is gone now," said Odin. "It won't be back."

Maeve frowned. "Oh, the goblins, once they have found a human to latch onto, will always come back."

"But we killed it," I said. "It can't possibly come back."

"Others will return in its <u>stead</u>," responded Maeve. "There are always others."

"But why is it my boy? Why have they chosen him?" I asked.

Maeve shrugged. "I am not entirely sure, but I think some boys and girls have more dreams than others, good dreams that the goblins like to feed upon."

"But our boy is suffering. He can't sleep at night, and he cries before bed. Isn't there a way to stop them?" inquired Odin.

The Dream Thief

Maeve shook her head. "Not that I know of."

Odin growled, his hackles rising. "Then I suppose we will have to continue killing them until they stop."

"Maeve's expression was one of sadness. "Death is a terrible thing for any creature. Why would you do such a thing?"

"Because it is hurting our boy, and we will not stand still while the one we love is harmed by evil <u>denizens</u> from your horrible land," I answered. I then turned to leave, going back into the tunnel from whence we had come. Odin started to follow.

"Wait!"

Odin and I turned back to Maeve.

"Let me try and help you," she said. "I will ask my mother if she knows about anything you can do to stop the goblins from returning. I will come to you within the next few nights with an answer."

"Thank you," I replied. We will be waiting."

T.R. Ross

Chapter 9

Odin and I kept watch. Nothing happened that night, or the following one, and Sam slept a restful sleep. We began to think that perhaps the fairy princess was wrong, and that the goblins wouldn't return after all. We abandoned our place in the closet, and Odin went back to sleeping wherever he chose around the house. I returned to my place on Sam's bed, sleeping humped over his feet to keep them warm in the darkest hours of the night.

And Maeve never came.

I don't know how many nights passed this way. Maybe three. Maybe four. And then, one night, I awoke to a sound. I looked in the direction from which it came, toward the crack of darkness that was the slightly open door that led into the hallway.

Ears pricked forward, I listened. *Thump, thump, thump.* The sound came again, from outside in the hallway, like something was tapping against the wall. I sprang from my spot and rushed to the door. I stuck my head out the crack and looked into the hallway...

To find nothing.

I crouched there for several moments, waiting to see if I would hear the sound again. Nothing. Finally, I rose and moved back into the room. I was about to jump back up onto the bed, when I heard it again. *Thump, thump, thump.* I spun around and rushed back to the door, this time entering the hallway.

There was nothing there. I sat back onto my haunches, confused. I knew I'd heard something. I heard a creaking sound, followed by "*snick*". I turned around to find that the door had shut behind me.

My hackles rose, and the hairs on my tail puffed out. I patted at the door, uncertain how it had closed. And it was then I heard it, a moaning from inside the bedroom. It was my boy, and he was having another nightmare.

"Mrow!" I called out to Sam, hoping he would awaken and let me back in. I heard him cry out, and I knew it was a terribly bad nightmare this time. Desperation entered my voice. "Mrow!"

The Dream Thief

Then he screamed. I leapt at the door, scratching at it. I continued to call out to him, hoping he would just wake up. He screamed again.

Ma and Dad burst from their room down the hall, followed by Odin who must have been sleeping in the basket of clothes that had still been warm from the dryer when the night began. Dad picked me up as Ma swung open the door and turned on the light. Sam was sitting up in bed, tears streaming down his flushed face. Ma rushed over to hug him, Dad following behind.

I glanced around the room, and when I saw nothing amiss, I looked up towards the hole in the ceiling. I caught a glimpse of glowing red eyes just before the hole closed as though it was never there.

T.R. ROSS

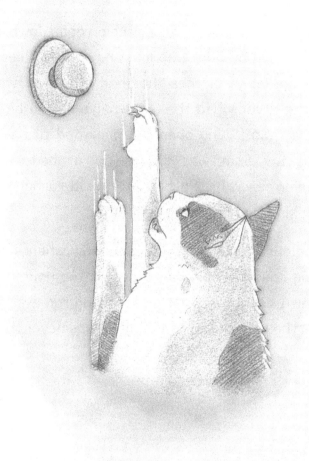

Chapter 10

"We will just have to remain vigilant again during the night," said Odin. "We can sleep during the day when the children are at school."

"We?" I asked. "So, you will help me?"

Odin's whiskers twitched in amusement. "Yes, I will help you, little scaredy cat."

I narrowed my eyes into slits. "I am not afraid. I can do it without you."

"Calm down, darling. I am just teasing you."

Not for the first time, I <u>bristled</u> at his choice of words. I am not, and never would be, anyone's darling. However, I chose to ignore him. "Maybe we should go back and see Maeve. She said she might be able to help us."

"She said she would come to us. Since she hasn't, I assume she doesn't have an answer," he said.

I was thoughtful for a moment. "I still think we should go see her, just in case."

Odin regarded me intently, saw that I wasn't about to let this go. "Fine, if she doesn't come to us by noon tomorrow, we will go."

I instantly felt better. "Thank you."

Odin rose from his place beside me in front of the fireplace. "Come, it is almost Sam's bedtime."

And so, it was. Ma's voice rang through the house as she <u>corralled</u> the four youngest children upstairs to put on their pajamas and brush their teeth. They then all went to their individual rooms. Meanwhile, the four oldest stayed on the main level of the house, where two large rooms housed two girls in one and two boys in the other. I had yet to explore them to my satisfaction, but thus far I enjoyed the multitudes of things on the floor that I could play with, and the piles of clothes I could burrow into.

It wasn't long before the house was quiet. Odin and I curled up at the foot of Sam's bed. The boy was <u>giddy</u> with happiness to have us there. I liked to think it was because he felt safer. Darkness settled around us, the pale light of the moon filtering in through the window blinds. The minutes ticked by and my eyelids began to droop. It had been a long day, and the warmth of Odin there beside me only served to increase my comfort. But I knew I couldn't doze very deeply, for the goblins had proven to be light of foot, slinking about in the shadows with <u>nary</u> a sound.

It was Odin who heard it first, and he nudged me gently to get my attention. A tinkling noise <u>emanated</u> from up near the ceiling where the hole liked to appear. And then I saw it, the shimmering outline of a pair of gossamer wings. Maeve had finally come.

She was small, tiny actually, barely the size of Sam's palm. As she fluttered closer, she grew in size until she was the size she appeared when we first met her. Wordlessly, she reached out to give us both a friendly pat, then moved towards the door. We followed behind, slipping through the crack and into the hallway.

"We shouldn't leave Sam alone," I said. "The goblins might come."

Maeve shook her head, speaking in a whisper. "They won't tonight. I sealed the hole after myself so that nothing can follow."

"Can you always do that?" asked Odin.

"No, not always. Only when I am present. I cannot leave the house lest the hole become unsealed again."

"Do you have an answer to our dilemma?" I asked.

"I do. My mother says a dreamcatcher will work against the goblins."

"A dreamcatcher? What is that?" inquired Odin.

"It is a protective charm used to turn away harm or powers of evil," Maeve explained. "It is a handmade willow hoop within which a net is woven, like a spider web. It is placed above a child's bed to protect them from nightmares. My mother says that the goblins do not like the magic inherent in them, and that they will leave your boy alone once he has one."

The Dream Thief

I was overcome with joy. "So, how do we get one of these dreamcatchers?"

Maeve smiled. "We must go to the Amazon."

Chapter 11

Odin and I perched on the desk while Maeve seated herself before the glowing screen that Alex always liked to look at so often. "My mother has taught me a little bit about how to use computers," said Maeve. "It will take us to the Amazon, where people like to buy things." She tapped her fingers along the keyboard. Images flowed across the screen, some familiar, some not. Before long, we came to what we were looking for. "This is it. This is a dreamcatcher."

It was a circle. In the center was the web that Maeve had described earlier, and caught within that web were beads and feathers of different shapes, colors, and sizes. Dangling from the circle were even more beads and feathers. I looked at it askance. "How does it work?"

"It is said that the bad dreams get caught in the web while the good dreams pass through," replied Maeve.

My whiskers twitched. "Alright, but how does that get rid of the goblins?"

"My mother says that the goblins are repulsed by the magic of the dreamcatchers," said Maeve.

Odin gave a sniff. "Well, this all sounds like a great idea, but all I see is a picture. How do we get one of these dreamcatchers here?"

Maeve turned to look at him, the light from the screen giving her beautiful face an <u>ethereal</u> glow. "That is the hard part. You must find a way to get your humans to discover this charm and bring it here from the Amazon."

Odin and I looked at one another, our minds racing to find a way to do that. It wasn't possible to simply tell them, for humans could not understand cat-speak. Sometimes they seemed to understand, but that was only if we were hungry, or if we weren't feeling well.

"I think we leave the picture up here on Alex's screen. Out of everyone in the house, he will be the one to investigate how it got there, and he will be the most likely one to read about it," said Odin.

"Do you think he will tell Ma about it?" I asked.

The Dream Thief

Odin was thoughtful. "I believe he will tell Arianna about it. Arianna will tell Ma."

Arianna was one of the girls, the one that I had learned was closest to Alex in age and temperament. They were often inseparable. Arianna also seemed to have a very close relationship with Ma, and would tell her anything. "I think you are right. Arianna would be the one to tell Ma, and then Ma will tell Dad."

Odin rose from his place. "It is settled then."

The rest of the night passed uneventfully before morning flew in upon the rays of a newly rising sun. Sam was still sleeping as Odin sauntered into the room, jumping up to sit beside me on the comforter at the foot of the bed.

I regarded the large tom intently, and when he didn't say anything, I spoke up. "Well?"

Odin's whiskers twitched. "Impatient, are we?"

I narrowed my eyes. I wasn't in the mood to play games. Sensing that, Odin continued. "It worked. Alex read all about the dreamcatcher, and even looked for more pictures of it."

Excitement rippled along my spine. We had done it! We had saved my boy! "Did he show it to Arianna?"

Odin's demeanor saddened. "No, he moved along to the other things he usually looks at."

Deflated, I turned away from him and lay down with my head on my paws. All that work, and it was for nothing. I felt a sense of hopelessness, much like I had felt at the end of my last life, in a home I'd lived in with another boy, the one with blond hair.

After a moment I felt a tap on my shoulder. "Freya, it doesn't mean he won't tell her about it sometime."

I looked back up at Odin. "What if Alex never tells Arianna? What then?" I asked.

His gaze became intense. "Then we keep fighting. Sam is worth that much, don't you think?"

The Dream Thief

Shame instantly flooded me. Odin was right. We would continue to fight until the battle was finally won. Sam was worth that much, and more. I looked over at my boy, soundly sleeping. I rose from my spot, moved to position myself at the curve of his belly and lay down again.

It was a place I wanted to always be.

Chapter 12

The nights passed, and it was just like Maeve said it would be. The goblins kept coming. While I guarded Sam, Odin kept vigil at the very top of the bookshelf on the desk, right below the hole. Their jibbering voices on the other side grated against our ears, enough that it made the hairs on our backs and tails stand on end for most of the night. But, knowing we were waiting for them, they never came through.

During the day, while the children were at school, we lay beside the fireplace and just slept, exhausted. The afternoons were harder, for there was much more distraction. But still, every night, we remained vigilant.

And Sam's nightmares went away.

Crisp autumn days became colder. The family dug out sweaters, footed pajamas, and winter blankets from out of storage. I looked out the window and watched the last leaves fall from the trees as fat white flakes fell from the sky. The children were excited by the sight, and when the flakes formed a blanket of shimmering white on the ground, they all stayed home from school and sat around playing games.

That night got cold in the house. I lay close to Sam and sadly looked up to where Odin sat alone on the high bookshelf. I was tempted to call him down, to tell him to come and curl up in the comfort of the thick blanket, but I held my tongue. Sam needed us to keep our nocturnal vigil so that he could sleep without fear. He was so much happier now without the nightmares; everyone could tell. He smiled wider, his eyes were brighter, and he chattered more at the dinner table. Ma had even said that his grades at school were better than they had ever been.

It was in the wee hours of the morning when I first heard something. Odin heard it too, his golden eye looking towards the cracked doorway from whence the sound had come. We waited, and when we heard it again, a scratching from somewhere outside the room, we both tensed. I rose from my place, giving Odin a glance before leaping down from the bed. He would stay and keep watch over Sam while I went to investigate.

I heard the noise yet again as I slipped out of the bedroom, coming from the direction of the staircase. I soundlessly made my way there, and followed it down the stairs to the first floor. For a moment there was nothing but silence, an uncanny silence that made the hairs on my back and tail stand at attention. *Something is watching me...*

And it was at that moment I heard a familiar jibbering, not just from in front of me, but also from *BEHIND*.

I instinctively lurched to the side as a ruby-eyed shadow careened past, just barely missing me. I growled and leapt after it, barely able to keep it in my sight as it scuttled away with supernatural speed. I <u>honed</u> in on it as it passed beneath the rays of moonlight streaming through the window blinds, and just as I was about to catch it, something barreled into me from my left.

The impact left me <u>sprawling</u> on the living room floor. The weight of it on my back kept me down as clawed hands dug into the fur around my neck, digging through the thick mane to the flesh beneath. I hissed as they dug deeper, deeper, until they punctured the skin, and then I yowled in pain. I scrambled to my feet and tore through the room, cackling laughter in my ear urging me faster and faster. The pain in my neck kept me going: over the table, across the sofa, and finally under the rocking chair in the hopes of dislodging the goblin. It held on with a <u>tenacious</u> grip, its claws sinking even deeper into my flesh, and terror infused my every pore.

My feet had wings as I dashed across the hall and into the kitchen. I slipped over the smooth tiled floor, barely dodging the legs of the table, the chairs, the trashcan, and finally ended up smashing into the island of cabinets in the center. With the weight suddenly lifted from my back, I was able to swiftly recover, leapt onto the nearest chair and then onto the table. In my headlong flight, I knocked over glasses left over from dinner. The loud sound of them crashing to the floor only increased my fear, and I swerved back around, going back across the table, and leapt again...

The Dream Thief

I was weightless. I had never attempted a jump so far. I landed onto the countertop of the island of cabinets and continued across, knocking the weekly mail, more glasses, and the fruit bowl onto the floor with a resounding crash. And it was then the lights flicked on.

I abruptly stopped, looking to the entryway of the kitchen. There stood Ma and Dad, expressions of shock on their faces. I leapt down from the island, shaking so badly that I barely landed on my feet, and bleated. "Mrrrowww!"

"Dear Lord Almighty! Look at this mess!" exclaimed Ma. "Freya, what have you done?"

I heard the disapproval in her voice, tinged with anger, and I crouched low to the ground. Dad just gave a gusty sigh and began to pick up shards of glass from the floor. Arianna slipped up behind Ma, her brown eyes wide with astonishment, her mouth in the shape of an O. And behind her were the other children, all in varying stages of wakefulness.

"Stay out of the kitchen, everyone. There's glass everywhere on the floor and you will cut your feet," said Dad.

Managing to avoid the glass, Ma stalked over to me. She bent down and I cried out in pain as she gripped my scruff, right where the goblin's talons had been. She picked me up and I cried again, yet I remained slack within her grip. "You have been a bad kitty, Freya! Bad Kitty!"

I closed my eyes at the indignity, at the pain, and mewled pathetically.

"What am I going to do with you?" She then walked back across the kitchen and deposited me into Arianna's arms. "Take her upstairs, Ari. I have a mess to help clean up."

The girl simply nodded and carried me into the dim hallway. I dejectedly looked over her shoulder as she carried me up the stairs, but something caught my eye.

In the deep shadows of the living room, on the far side of the sofa, I saw two flashes of glowing red.

The Dream Thief

Chapter 13

"It was an ambush." Odin's tone was deadpan.

I lay curled up on Sam's bed, my head on my forepaws, my neck throbbing with pain. I felt bad about myself, the mess I had made downstairs, and the worry I had caused the family.

"They must have gotten in during the day when we weren't keeping watch over the hole. I didn't know they could do that," he continued. Odin licked at my neck, only making it feel worse. But I didn't tell him to stop, as the wounds needed cleaning. "I heard the commotion downstairs, but I thought maybe you had it handled..."

I tensed. "There were two of them," I interrupted. "I didn't have it handled."

"Shhh," he whispered. "I know that now. I don't blame you." He paused in his grooming. "You are bleeding. I am surprised Ma didn't notice."

My heart sank as I recalled her disappointment. "She was very upset with me."

"It is still very unlike her," he said. "You know she still loves you."

Trepidation swept through me, followed by memories of my last home. They had left me outside one day and never came back. I must have done something wrong; I must have been a bad kitty. But, for the life of me, I didn't know what it was that I had done.

I started to tremble, fear coursing through me like a wild river. Thoughts of the unthinkable pervaded my mind, and I imagined Ma and Dad putting me outside into that cold blanket on the ground that stretched on like a sea of deadly whiteness.

"Shhh, hush my darling. You are safe here," whispered Odin in a soothing voice.

There it is again, that word. Darling. But this time it made me feel secure instead of irritated. Maybe I didn't mind being "darling" to someone, especially to someone who seemed to truly care about me. Even if he did call me a scaredy cat.

The Dream Thief

I snuggled closer to my good friend and closed my eyes. I was so very sore, and tired from my madcap dash through the house. Several moments later I felt Sam getting into bed and pulling the covers up to his chin. He put his hand on my head, trailed it down over my back and over my tail. "You are a good girl, Freya, chasing that bad Boogeyman for me," he said. "You are a good kitty."

And with those magical words, my trembling ceased. And I was content.

The next morning, the kids went to school, and Odin and I went hunting. The house was huge, much bigger than the one I had lived in before, so it took us quite a while. We searched the second floor first: all five bedrooms and two bathrooms. It was followed by the first floor: the two kids' bedrooms, kitchen, bathroom, study, and laundry room. We saved the living room for last, where I had first encountered the goblins the night before. We could smell them everywhere, especially in the farthest corner from the light, the one between the shelves around the television and the small table that rested beside the rocking chair. The place positively reeked of their foul stench, but not a single goblin could be found there.

It was only after we thoroughly searched every nook and cranny of the living room that we came to the <u>ominous</u> door off of the kitchen, the one that hardly anyone used. Usually it was closed, but today it was cracked open. Odin paused there and looked back at me. "It's time for the basement. Are you ready?"

I sat back on my haunches and regarded the cracked door. A <u>musty</u> smell emanated from it, one I didn't much like. "Basement? What's a basement?"

He regarded me intently. "It is a dark place, one I've <u>ventured</u> into only a few times myself. Dad goes down there every once in a while, and Ma."

I cocked my head. "But what IS it?"

"I believe it is meant to be a safe place. The family went down there once when there was a very bad storm. They took me with them, and the turtle in Sam's room."

The Dream Thief

"The little animal in that shell? It's called a turtle?" My whiskers twitched as I recalled the odd smell of the creature.

Odin's eye twinkled. "Yes."

I looked back towards the door. A shiver swept through me and I flicked my tail. "I get a strange feeling about this basement."

Odin pawed at the door. "Yes, but it is the one place we have yet to look."

I rose from my haunches just as Ma entered the kitchen from the laundry room, carrying a basket of freshly dried clothes. On her way past, she closed the basement door and headed into the hallway and up the stairs. Odin gave an unhappy rumble deep in his throat and sniffed. I just sat back on my haunches. A part of me was just as discontented as Odin, but the other part of me couldn't help feeling relieved.

Chapter 14

"But Maaaa! I wanna sleep with Freya! She always sleeps in my room!"

"Now Sammy, don't make this more difficult than it already is. She woke the whole house up last night, not to mention destroying the fruit bowl that my grandmother gave to me."

"She didn't mean it!" Sam pointed to me. "Look, she's already in my bed. She wants to stay. She will be lonely down there all by herself!"

Ma scooped me up off the bed and secured me under one arm. "Sam, I said no, and that is the end of this discussion. You can let Freya out in the morning when you get up for school."

Sam blinked rapidly, his brown eyes shiny with threatened tears. "Ma, please..."

"No, Sam. She will be waiting for you in the morning. Now get some sleep."

As Ma carried me from Sam's room, I saw my boy put his hands to his eyes. My heart <u>wrenched</u> and I squirmed in her grasp. She situated me more securely and carried me down the hall to the stairs. *Where are we going?*

My pulse began to race as we made our way down, and once at the foot of the stairs, turned left and into the kitchen. My chest bottomed out as she stopped at the door leading into the basement. *No. No, no, no...* "Mrow."

I heard Odin's voice behind us. "Freya, everything will be okay."

I looked back and saw him standing there, an expression of concern in his eyes. My body shook with fear and I squirmed again. "Odin! She's leaving me!"

"No, it's just for the night. Ma would never leave you!"

"I'm afraid!"

Ma opened the door and the musty smell streamed forth. She then began down the creaking staircase. Odin followed behind. "I know, but you will be fine, darling."

The Dream Thief

Once Ma reached the bottom of the stairs, she set me on a cushion. "Here is a bed for you, Freya," she said. Ma stroked my head and back lovingly before picking up Odin and making her way back up the stairs.

"Mrroww." I called after her, hoping she would stop. But she never did, and once at the top, she closed the door.

Darkness enveloped me and I just sat there on the cushion, staring until my eyes adjusted. The only light was that streaming from the narrow slit beneath the door. Within moments, I was back up the stairs. I put my paws against the door and called out. "Mrroww!"

I heard paws on the other side, Odin trying to get to me. "Freya!"

"Odin!" My voice was panicked. "Tell them to let me out!"

I heard him on the other side of the door, calling out. "Mrow! Mrow!" Then his paws were at the door again, a sweeping sound that brought me at least some comfort. I did the same, pawing desperately at the door, hoping that Ma would <u>recant</u> and let me back in. The basement was cold, and the air had a slight damp feeling to it. I hated it.

I don't know how long we did that: calling back and forth to one another and pawing at that door. It never opened, and after a while, the light streaming from beneath it turned off.

I sat there for several moments, <u>despondent</u>. I put my nose to the slit, smelled Odin still sitting there on the other side. He shouldn't be there; Sam needed him to keep the goblins away. But I knew that might not work anymore. The goblins had entered the house in the light of day, had managed to ambush me and get me locked up down here in the basement. Odin may have been a match against two of them with his size, but more than that, and he would be quickly overcome, just as I had been.

"Odin?"

"Yes, darling. I am right here."

"You should go to Sam. He needs you."

The Dream Thief

"No, I am staying here with you. You need me more."

I put my nose to the slit once again, felt Odin doing the same when I felt the slightest touch of his breath. "Odin, please..."

"No." His voice was <u>adamant</u>. "Sam might be your boy, but you are my Freya. You are to me what Sam is to you. I will not leave you."

Chapter 15

The hours ticked by as I lay there on the top step by the door. I would look at the steps, stretching downward as though into a yawning pit, and cringe. The shadows were deep, and so dark I wondered if even my superior feline vision would be able to see there. At the bottom lay my bed, a forlorn cushion <u>festooned</u> with pawprints on a bright purple background. It looked lonely, just like I felt, and I was sad. The only thing that kept me going was the presence of Odin on the other side of the door, and a feeling of security would wash away the sadness. There was someone who cared for me more than any other, and for that I was grateful.

A sudden sound from the pit below thrust me into immediate alertness. It was like something I'd never heard before, almost like a low moan followed by a distant <u>cackle</u>. It set the hairs along my spine to standing, and I pinned my ears back and hissed. The air felt suddenly heavy, and it felt like something was down there, something *wrong*.

"Freya?"

Odin's voice took me out of the moment and I turned towards the door.

"Freya, are you there?"

My voice shook. "Odin, there is something down here."

His tone shifted to one of alarm. "What?"

"Something is down here."

"Like a goblin?"

"No, something else." I gathered my resolve and stood up. "I am going to see what it is."

I heard him suddenly start pawing at the door again. "No, you should stay right here."

I was tempted to do as Odin proposed, stay in my spot on the top step in the security of his presence on the other side of the door. But if there was really something in the bowels of the basement, I needed to know. My boy depended on me for protection. How could I protect him if I didn't know what I was protecting him against?

The Dream Thief

"I need to look. I will be back." And with that, I stepped downward.

The stairs seemed longer going down than they did going up. The darkness surrounded me in an oppressive veil, but I found that I could still see just as well as I did on the top step. I slowly ventured forth into the depths of the basement, the hard floor cold beneath my paws. I moved deeper and deeper, passing stacks of tattered boxes, old furniture, and a mess of other things strewn here and there. Faint traces of moonlight filtered in through small glass block windows near the ceiling, obscured by ancient spider webs sagging with dust.

I turned a corner and found myself in another room of the basement. It, too, was filled with old, forgotten things, and it was like no one had stepped foot there in decades. Here the oppression was more palpable, the heaviness in the air weighing me down so much that I slowed my pace. It was colder here; I could tell in spite of my thick fur. And the wrongness I had felt at the top of the stairs was more potent here.

Once again, my hackles rose. I sniffed at the stale air and suddenly the wrongness had a smell to it. It reminded me of the goblins, but it wasn't the same. I followed the scent and it got stronger and stronger. I followed it to the far wall, and then it suddenly stopped.

I looked around: up, down, and around. To the left was a dilapidated bookshelf. It had toppled over, and the top edge of it leaned against the wall. I sniffed in that direction and went towards it, the scent of wrongness getting stronger again. When I reached it, I paused.

It was dark in that space the shelf made where it leaned against the wall, darker than anywhere else in the basement. The sensation I got when I looked at it made my skin crawl. A part of me didn't want to go in, sensing that the wrongness emanating from the place was dangerous. But the other part of me was <u>compelled</u>. I had come too far to turn back now, and somehow, I knew I'd find what I had been searching for.

Slowly, I crept towards the opening. The pitch blackness within encompassed me, and even my

The Dream Thief

feline vision struggled for a moment. The wrongness here was <u>pervasive</u>, and it shook me to my core. Trembling in fear, I moved deeper, step by hesitant step. Every sense was on the highest alert.

The ground became rocky, strange since the rest of the basement was flat floor. I examined the rocks beneath my feet and found that they were all white, and polished smooth, about the size of my toe-pads. I batted at one with my forepaw, examining it this way and that. It wasn't completely round, rather a bit misshapen. I swatted it and it skittered across the floor and out beyond the opening. I moved deeper and the rocks became more <u>proliferative</u>, until suddenly I was faced with an entire pile of them, one that was as high as I stood tall.

For a few moments I just stood there and looked at the pile of oddly shaped stones. It seemed strange that they were all just lying there, as though placed there by someone, hidden there beneath this old bookshelf. I looked all around the pile, examined more of the rocks. Some were bigger, some smaller, all polished white. There was something familiar about them...

And it was then I knew. I knew what they were. They were familiar because I looked at them every day within the mouths of the humans we lived with.

They were teeth.

The Dream Thief

Chapter 16

For the rest of the night, I lay with my side pressed against the door at the top of the stairs. Odin tried talking to me, but I just lay there, frightened. Early in the morning, Sam came down to open the door. I rushed into his waiting arms and trembled as he held me close. I breathed in his scent, just happy to be with him again.

After the children went to school, Odin sat with me in the comfort of Sam's room. "Did Sam have a nightmare last night?" I asked.

"Yes," he replied sadly.

I slumped dejectedly into the blankets. A few moments of silence passed. "I noticed you didn't eat your food this morning." His tone filled with worry. "Did something happen in the basement? Are you sick?"

I gazed at him through unblinking eyes. "I hate that place. But I will be <u>consigned</u> to it once again tonight, I imagine."

Much to my relief, he didn't ask anything more about it, just lay there thoughtfully, his side pressed against mine. We slept for most of the day, and when the children came home from school, I sat with Sam for as long as I could. When it was bedtime, Ma gently picked me up from the blankets. Sam instantly started to cry.

"Ma, no! Don't take her away!"

Ma's voice was sad. "Now, Sam, you know I have to."

Fat tears rolled down his cheeks. "But I miss her! And she keeps the Boogeyman away!"

"Sammy, there is no such thing as the Boogeyman," said Alex wryly as he walked into the bedroom.

"Yes, there is!" Sam shouted. "I've seen him myself!"

Alex furrowed his brows into a frown. "I thought you said that Freya and Odin killed the Boogeyman. If he is dead, how can he still be here?"

The Dream Thief

Sam scrunched his face into an angry scowl. "Shut up, Alex!"

"Sam, cut it out!" said Ma. "Alex is right. There are no such things as Boogeymen. You are just having bad dreams."

"Then why are the dreams gone when Freya is with me?" Sam retorted.

Ma gave a deep sigh.

"Actually," said Arianna entering the room behind Alex, "I have read that cats can ward off evil spirits."

Sam looked up at the older girl hopefully.

"Where did you read that?" asked Alex.

Arianna came over to me and petted the top of my head. I purred in appreciation. "On the internet."

Alex nodded thoughtfully. "You will have to show me that sometime." His eyes lit up. "I actually read about something else on the internet. It's called a dreamcatcher."

Ma and Arianna both nodded. "Yes, many Native Americans used them to protect children from bad dreams and evil spirits," said Ma.

Arianna hopped up and down excitedly. "We studied about Native Americans at school and our class made some dreamcatchers!"

Ma smiled. "When was this?"

"Just a couple of weeks ago!"

Alex smiled. "Maybe you could bring one home for Sam."

"They are hanging up in the hallway right now, but I can ask my teacher."

A rush of relief swept over me. Finally, finally there was going to be help!

Arianna's eyes sparkled. "I put a lot of love into mine. Our teacher brought in some really nice things and it looks just like the ones in the books she gave us to look at!"

Ma looked at Sam. "What do you think about that?"

The Dream Thief

The boy wiped the tears from his eyes and nodded enthusiastically.

"And since cats also keep evil spirits away, we should let Freya stay here with Sam," said Arianna, her tone hopeful.

Ma gave another <u>gusty</u> sigh. "I don't know, Ari. She caused a lot of destruction downstairs the other night."

"Why don't you just close her into Sam's room so she can't get out?" she asked.

Ma gave a <u>resigned</u> nod. "Alright, but if she causes trouble, she out." She turned to Sam. "Do you understand?"

"Yes, Ma! She's going to lay right here in bed with me, aren't you girl?" The boy reached out his arms and Ma released me into them. He crushed me to his chest and I gave a little squeak.

Everyone filed out of the room. Arianna turned to smile at Sam and I as she closed the door behind her. My gratitude went out to the girl. Because of

Arianna, I had been promoted back into the house again. My basement confinement was over.

The Dream Thief

Chapter 17

Odin had pawed at the door until Sam let him in. Now we both lay there at the foot of the bed and waited for the boy to fall asleep. It wasn't long before Odin was <u>resuming</u> his position at the top of the bookcase, and I at the small of Sam's back. And not long after that, we started hearing sounds outside of the room. Only this time, we weren't falling for that trick, not to mention, the door was closed and there was no way for us to get out anyways.

The jibbering at the mouth of the hole was loud. Both Odin and I sat there with tense expectancy, waiting, waiting, waiting...

Until a hush suddenly fell over the room, a heavy hush that made me feel like we were inside some kind of bubble. And then a goblin burst forth from the hole and landed on top of Odin.

"Rawwwrrr!" Odin screeched like a demon from hell, hissing and clawing. And as the two scrambled about on the top ledge of the bookshelf, a second goblin emerged from the hole, followed by a third wearing a glowing blue <u>amulet</u> around its neck. I had barely a chance to glance over at Sam before I dashed off to meet the threat, and was shocked to find that Sam hadn't moved, as though he hadn't heard a thing.

With the grace of a ninja from one of those movies the boys liked to watch, the second goblin leapt at the same time I did. We met in midair between the bed and the shelf, falling to the floor in a tangle of legs. I narrowly missed biting down on one arm while the goblin raked its clawed hand over my face. I barely closed my eyes in time, felt the sting of parting flesh, and yowled. I lost my grip entirely, and it took the advantage and climbed over onto my back where it was hard for me to reach it.

Memories of the other night rushed through my mind, and I knew I couldn't make a repeat performance. Instead, I gathered all my strength in my hind legs and made a rush for the small space beneath the dresser. I, alone, would fit. The goblin...

The Dream Thief

Thunk! I felt the goblin become unseated as I squeezed beneath the dresser. I made a quick turn and saw it lying on the floor. Quickly, before it could gather it's wits, I grabbed its foot. My teeth punctured its flesh and it cried out as my tongue tasted the putrid flavor of its blood. I gagged and almost let go, but I gathered my will to hang on, dragging it beneath the dresser with me.

It was there I left it, swiftly sliding back out into the open. In the background I could hear the continued struggle between Odin and the first goblin, but my sights were set on Sam.

The boy was in the throes of another nightmare, the third goblin hovering over him. Sam's mouth was open in a silent scream, the pale yellow glow leaving to enter the goblin's open maw. The blue amulet glowed brightly, pulsing with some inner radiance.

The goblin didn't see me coming.

I leapt onto it's back, immediately going for its throat. The goblin fell forward onto Sam and my heart skipped a beat. I sank my teeth in deep, then pulled back to get the foul thing off of my boy. A hideous shriek filled the room, followed by a scream of terror from Sam. I pulled back, back, back, sinking my teeth ever deeper. The goblin writhed within my grip as its blood pumped into my mouth and dribbled down my chin.

And then I was struck from behind, and I remembered the second goblin I had left beneath the dresser.

Sam screamed again. I growled around the third goblin's throat and bucked to dislodge the second one. It was heavy and it clawed at the side of my face, trying to get me off of its comrade. But I refused to let go; I COULDN'T let go. If I did, it would run off and be free to attack us another night. The razor-sharp claws raked my face, almost taking out my eye. I hung onto the third goblin with all that was in me...

A third scream from Sam and suddenly the second goblin was gone. The third goblin had ceased resisting and it hung limply in my jaws. I shook it roughly for good measure, and sensing the life had left it, I dropped its body. I swiftly turned to see Odin doing the same thing, dropping the lifeless body of the second goblin at his feet. Gashes covered his face, and the fur around his neck was matted with blood, but he stood tall and proud. The sound of Sam's sobbing cries bade us rush to his side...

The light from the third goblin's amulet dulled and went out. The heavy hush that had pervaded the room during our struggles suddenly lifted.

Sam scooped me up in his arms. "Oh, Freya, I was so afraid for you!" He reached for Odin and brought him close too. "Odin, you are such a strong boy! You are such a hero!" He sobbed uncontrollably, holding us so tight I could feel his love as a physical thing. I licked his face, tasting the salty tears he shed for us, and my heart swelled.

Suddenly the lights clicked on and another scream resounded throughout the room, followed by, "Oh my God!" It was Ma, her eyes wide with fright. Dad came up behind her and rushed into the room. He swept Sam up off the bed and handed the boy off to her. Odin and I just sat there, stock still, as Dad assessed the room. He went to the other side of the bed and looked down at the floor, his head shaking.

"Where the heck are these rats coming from?"

"Dear, look at the cats! Their faces are all cut, up and they are covered in blood!" said Ma.

Dad came over to us, patted each of our heads, and took a closer look. "Yes, they need to see the vet. Those wounds need to be cleaned, and some may need to be stitched."

Ma nodded. "I will get the van started."

The Dream Thief

Chapter 18

A familiar medicinal smell filled my nostrils as we left the cold, dark outdoors and entered the brightly lit building. I shrank into the back of my small space and trembled, the memories of the last time I'd smelled such a place rushing through my mind. I remembered the pain, the smell of blood, and the tiny kittens that finally came. Despite all my efforts to clean them, to care for them, they never awoke from their peaceful sleep. I cried for them when the humans came to take them away, and I never saw them again.

We were immediately taken back into a room, and once there, the doors to our spaces were opened. Ma's soothing voice coaxed me out, and once in her arms, I wrapped my paws around her neck and cried, "Mrow! *(Please don't leave me here!)*"

"Hush, darling," said Odin. "Everything will be alright. We aren't getting left here." Despite his own trembling, his voice seemed so certain. I wanted to believe him, but I was so afraid.

A man with a white coat came into the room and he looked us both over with calm <u>efficiency</u>. "We can have these wounds cleaned right away," he said. "Now what was it you said happened?"

"They killed three rats that somehow got into the house," said Ma.

The vet shook his head. "That's strange, because these don't look like wounds that a cat would get from a fight with a rat."

Ma's brows <u>furrowed</u>. "What do they look like they are from, then?"

The vet shrugged. "I'm not sure, but not a rat."

Odin and I were put back into our spaces and carried into another room. The medicinal smell was even stronger here, and my body shook where I crouched as far back into my space as I could get. When I wouldn't come out of my own accord, firm hands reached in and brought me out. The floor beneath my paws was shiny grey, and cold. I looked around for Odin, but I couldn't see him.

The Dream Thief

"Mrrroww!" I called out to him.

"Hush, pretty girl," said an unfamiliar feminine voice. A gentle hand ran over my fur. "We are going to take good care of you." A sudden prick to the side of my neck made me cry out, and within moments the room began to spin.

Then there was only darkness.

I awoke laying in Ma's lap, her arms around me. The familiar drone told me that we were going somewhere. I was tired, so very tired, and I felt my eyelids droop before I remembered. "Odin? Odin, are you here?" I called out.

"Freya? I'm here." His voice sounded tired, slurred almost, and I wondered if mine sounded the same.

Before I knew it, we were being carried into the house and the doors to our spaces opened. Sam was right there, picking me up and cradling me in his arms. "Ma, Freya looks like she was hurt really bad!"

"She will be alright, Sammy. The doctor shaved her fur so he could clean the cuts. He had to stitch some of them too. See?" Ma pointed to a place on my neck where the goblins had dug their claws in deep. "She has medicine to take, and she will get better," Ma continued.

"I will take care of you, girl," Sam whispered into my ear. He squeezed me ever so gently. "I'll take care of you just like you take care of me."

The Dream Thief

Chapter 19

All that day, Odin and I slept by the warmth of the fire, waiting for the children to get home from school. He looked a bit worse for wear, his fur shaved around his neck and shoulders, and even one spot on his hindquarters where he'd been bitten. He said I looked much the same, but worse, because my hair was so much longer than his and made the shaved areas look so <u>stark</u>.

Sitting face-to-face, my gaze roved over his features and it stopped over the place where his second eye should have been. The socket was closed shut, with a slightly puckered look, and had fur growing there.

"Odin," I asked, "how did you lose your eye?"

He regarded me intently. "I don't know. I don't remember I time when I had two. Maybe I was born this way." He cocked his head. "Does it bother you?"

If cats could smile, I would have. "No, I like you just the way you are."

Odin's remaining eye twinkled, and slowly, ever so slowly, he touched his nose to mine. It was a loving kiss, sweeter than I'd ever imagined one could be, and I touched my nose to his in return. It brought to mind the words he had spoken to me when I was in the basement, words spoken through the closed door between us: *"You are my Freya. You are to me what Sam is to you."*

I settled closer to Odin and closed my eyes, content to be in his presence. We <u>basked</u> in the heat of the fire, on the bed Ma had brought up out of the cold basement. I'd never told him about the weird pile of teeth I'd found; It simply didn't seem significant in the press of other, more important things.

There was a flurry of activity when the children returned home. Odin and I watched them in tense anticipation, and when Arianna walked in carrying her prize, we rose from our places and went to see what would happen.

"Oh, Ari! This looks so beautiful, just like the ones I've seen in stores!" gushed Ma.

The Dream Thief

Arianna beamed at the praise. "Our teacher is part Native American and she brought in the willow hoops for us to use. She taught us how to make the webs and provided all kinds of things to put in them. See, I have beads, feathers, and even a <u>shard</u> of bone! I like purple, so I have that color as my theme."

I looked up at the dreamcatcher, and it really did look like the ones Odin an I had seen on the internet. It was bigger than I thought it would be, the <u>diameter</u> of the hoop at least as long as I was.

"So, where are we going to hang it?" asked Alex and Todd in unison.

"Let's put it over Sam's bed," said Ma. "There's a nice empty space there."

While the children trooped upstairs, Ma got a hammer and nail. Once in Sam's room, Ma stood on the bed, positioned the dreamcatcher just right, and hammered the nail into the wall. All of the children gave a cheer.

After everyone had left, Odin and I sat on the bed, admiring the dreamcatcher. It looked perfect where Ma had hung it, right over the place where Sam slept every night. I looked at my companion and saw a question burning in his eyes, the same one that was in mine: would the dreamcatcher keep the goblins away?

The Dream Thief

Chapter 20

It was late. The family had gone to bed hours ago and Odin and I sat in our old spot in Sam's closet. We knew it was dangerous to stay, but, sore and tired as we were, we couldn't just leave Sam alone without knowing if the dreamcatcher would work. So, we waited, and waited, and waited. Then we waited some more.

We heard the jibbering before we saw the hole open. It remained that way for several moments before the goblins decided that Odin really wasn't there guarding it anymore, and then started to climb out. The moonlight, obscured by clouds, was thin where it came in through the blinds in the window, making it more difficult to see. But it was easy to tell that multiple shadows crept about the room, all looking for the peril that Sam's two feline protectors imposed. The goblins chuckled among themselves, perhaps imagining that our injuries kept us away.

One of the goblins had an amulet around its neck, just like the one from the night before. It pulsed with a blue glow, and the familiar hush fell over the place. I imagined it kept those on the outside from hearing what was going on inside the room.

I kept looking at the dreamcatcher where it hung above the bed. It remained lifeless, just a thing suspended on the wall. I shifted restlessly, compelled to do something, but Odin's paw over mine kept me there.

Then it happened. A shadow born of the darkest, most vile of places climbed up onto the bed beside Sam. The goblin hovered over him, reached out a clawed hand to turn the boy's face toward it. My heart thumped against my ribs and I squirmed in my spot. Odin tensed beside me and I could sense that it was equally as difficult for him to just sit and wait without doing anything.

Sam began to moan in his sleep, his legs moving beneath the covers. The nightmare was beginning, and as it gathered force, he cried out...

Sam's mouth opened, and the goblin was there. The familiar golden glow began to issue forth, and

The Dream Thief

it was then the dreamcatcher flared to life. An intense purple glow highlighted the web and surrounding hoop, casting the entire room into stark relief. Five goblins surrounded the bed, the sixth positioned over my boy. A low hum filled the air, gathering in intensity. Before any of them could react, the glow in the shape of the web dissociated from the charm and rushed towards the goblins, enveloping them in its purple strands.

The goblins shrieked in agony. The web burned into their bodies, and we could hear the sizzling of flesh. The goblin beside Sam jumped down from the bed, and fast as lightning, streaked up the bookshelf and into the hole. The others followed swiftly behind, the purple strands sticking to them like glue. Once they were all through, the hush lifted from the room, and the hole disappeared like it had never been.

The room was quiet as Odin and I slunk out from the closet. Sam slept peacefully, his breaths deep and even. I jumped onto the bed and carefully went to where the dreamcatcher hung.

Once again, it looked like just another thing hanging on the wall, silent and still. I reached up to sniff it, and I sneezed when one of the feathers tickled my nose.

I felt Odin join me on the bed and turned back to see him sitting there, his tail wrapped around his forepaws. I went over and rubbed my side against his before settling down beside him. Odin did the same, laying down with me in the covers and snuggling in deep.

There we rested for the remainder of the night. And Sam had no nightmares.

The End

The Dream Thief

Glossary

abashed (adj) - embarrassed, disconcerted, or ashamed

abrupt (adj) - sudden and unexpected

accommodate (verb) - to adapt; to make room for

adamant (adj) - refusing to be persuaded or to change one's mind

affront (verb) - to offend the modesty or values of

amble (verb) - to walk or move at a slow, relaxed pace

ambush (noun) - a surprise attack by people lying in wait in a concealed position

amiss (adj) - not quite right; inappropriate or out of place

amulet (noun) - something that is worn or kept, typically as a necklace, to give magical protection

askance (adv) - with an attitude or look of suspicion or disapproval assail (verb) - to make a concerted or violent attack on

bask (verb) - to lie exposed in warmth and light, typically from the sun, for relaxation and pleasure

bristle (verb) - to become aggressive or angry

cackle (verb) - make a harsh, raucous sound when laughing

cacophony (noun) - a harsh, discordant mixture of sounds

canopy (noun) - a protective covering overhead

caustic (adj) - sarcastic in a scathing and bitter way

cavernous (adj) - like a cavern in size, shape, or atmosphere; giving the impression of vast, dark depths

cease (verb) - to bring or come to an end

chaos (noun) - complete disorder and confusion

The Dream Thief

compel (verb) - to force or oblige (someone) to do
   something

concession (noun) - a thing that is granted,
   especially in response to demands; a thing
   conceded

consign (verb) - to assign; commit decisively or
   permanently

corral (verb) - to gather together and confine

deadpan (adj) - deliberately impassive or
   expressionless

denizen (noun) - an inhabitant or occupant of a
   particular place

desperation (noun) - a state of despair, typically
   which results in rash or extreme behavior

despondent (adj) - in low spirits from loss of hope
   or courage

diameter (noun) - a straight line passing through
   the center of a body or figure, especially a
   circle or sphere

disdainful (adj) - showing contempt or lack of
    respect

dissociate (verb) - to disconnect or separate (used
    especially in abstract contexts)

distort (verb) - to pull or twist out of shape

drone (verb) - to make a continuous low humming
    sound

earnest (adj) - resulting from or showing sincere
    and intense conviction

efficiency (noun) - the ability to produce something
    with a minimum amount of effort

emanate (verb) - to give out or emit; to spread out
    from (something abstract but perceptible)

ethereal (adj) - extremely delicate and light in a
    way that seems too perfect for this world

festoon (verb) - to adorn with ribbons, garlands, or
    other decorations

The Dream Thief

furrow (verb) - to worry or puzzle over, to
concentrate so hard that lines appear on your
forehead

giddy (verb) - to make someone feel excited to the
point of disorientation

grasp (verb) - to seize and hold firmly

grimace (noun) - an ugly, twisted expression on a
person's face, typically expressing disgust,
pain, or wry amusement

gurgle (verb) - to make a hollow bubbling sound like
that made by water running out of a bottle

gusty (adj) - characterized by a sudden burst of
vigorous blowing

hasten (verb) - to be quick to do something

haunch (noun) - a buttock and thigh considered
together, in human or animal

hazel (noun) - a variation of brown eyes, only with
more green or gold in the iris

T.R. Ross

hone (verb) - to sharpen, refine, or perfect something over a period of time

inherent (adj) - existing in something as a permanent, essential, or characteristic attribute

intimidate (verb) - to frighten or put someone in awe, especially in order to make them do what one wants

jibber (verb) - to chatter so quickly as to make it almost difficult to understand

luxuriate (verb) - to enjoy oneself in a luxurious way; to take self-indulgent delight

maul (verb) - to wound a person or animal by scratching and tearing

mewl (verb) - to cry feebly or querulously; whimper

musty (adj) - having a stale, moldy, or damp smell

nary (adj) - nonstandard form of not

nestle (verb) - to settle or lie comfortably within or against something

The Dream Thief

nocturnal (adj) - done, occurring, or active at night

olfactory (adj) - relating to the sense of smell

ominous (adj) - giving the impression that something bad or unpleasant is going to happen; threatening; inauspicious

oppression (noun) - mental pressure or distress

ordeal (noun) - a painful or horrific ordeal, especially a one lasting a long time or longer than expected

palpable (adj) - (of a feeling or atmosphere) so intense it seems almost able to be physically touched

peril (noun) - serious and immediate danger

pervasive (adj) - (especially of an unwelcome influence or physical effect) spreading widely throughout an area or a group of people

pique (verb) - stimulate (interest or curiosity)

potent (adj) - having great power, influence, or effect

T.R. Ross

proliferative (adj) - rapidly growing and increasing in number

purchase (noun) - a hold or position on something for applying power advantageously

quizzical (adj) - (of a person's expression or behavior) indicating mild or amused puzzlement

recant (verb) - to withdraw or repudiate (a statement or belief) formally and publically; renounce

resume (verb) - begin to do or pursue something again after a pause or interruption

resigned (adj) - having accepted something unpleasant that one cannot do anything about

robust (adj) - strong and healthy; vigorous

ruckus (noun) - a disturbance or commotion

saunter (verb) - to walk in a slow, relaxed manner, without hurry or effort

The Dream Thief

shard (noun) - a piece of broken ceramic, metal, glass, or rock typically having sharp edges

spoils (noun) - goods stolen or taken forcibly from a person or place

sprawl (verb) - to sit, lie, or fall with one's arms and legs spread out in an awkward way

stark (adj) - severe or bare in appearance or outline

stead (noun) - the place or role that someone or something should have or fill (used in referring to a substitute)

tenacious (adj) - tending to keep a firm hold of something; clinging or adhering closely

tense (verb) - to make tight or rigid (especially of a muscle or someone's body)

tom (noun) - the male of various animals, especially a turkey or domestic cat

trepidation (noun) - a feeling of fear or agitation about something that may happen twain (adj) - archaic term for two

vacate (verb) - to leave (a place that was previously occupied)

vaccination (noun) - treatment with a vaccine to produce immunity against a disease; inoculation

vague (adj) - of uncertain, indefinite, or unclear character or meaning

vault (verb) - to leap or jump over while propelling oneself with arms or legs

venture (noun) - a risky or daring journey or undertaking

vivid (adj) - (of color) intensely deep or bright

waft (verb) - to pass or cause to pass easily or gently through or as if through the air

wince (verb) - to give a slight involuntary grimace or shrinking movement of the body out of or in anticipation of pain or distress

The Dream Thief

wrench (verb) - to pull or twist (someone or
   something) suddenly and violently

wry (adj) - using or expressing dry, especially
   mocking, humor

About the Author

Tracy R. Ross lives in Cincinnati, Ohio with her husband, six children, four cats, two ferrets and one dog. Growing up, she always loved animals and writing, and she is happy to finally be able to combine the two in her new book series. She also loves eating pizza, smelling the air after it rains, vacations in the mountains, meeting and talking with her readers, and, of course, petting her cats!

About the Illustrator

Miriam Chowdhury is 20 years old and lives in Cincinnati, Ohio. She is currently working full-time in retail while taking college classes in order to pursue art education. Her hobbies include drawing, photography, and taekwondo. Some of her favorite things to watch are anime and horror movies; however, she doesn't like the dark and spiders! She has a really big sweet tooth, but the things she loves most in life are spending time with friends and family, making art, and cuddling with her kitty.